Halloween Hats

NOV 0 4 2002

Elizabeth Winthrop

Halloween Hats

illustrated by
Sue Truesdell

Henry Holt and Company
New York

Henry Holt and Company, LLC
Publishers since 1866
115 West 18th Street
New York, New York 10011
www.henryholt.com

Library of Congress Cataloging-in-Publication Data
Winthrop, Elizabeth.
Halloween hats / Elizabeth Winthrop; illustrated by Sue Truesdell.
Summary: A rhyming celebration of hats that help create costumes for the Halloween parade.
[1. Hats—Fiction. 2. Halloween—Fiction. 3. Parades—Fiction.
4. Stories in rhyme.] I. Truesdell, Sue, ill. II. Title.
PZ8.3.W727 Hal 2002   [E]—dc21   2001005203

ISBN 0-8050-6386-2
First Edition—2002
Printed in the United States of America on acid-free paper. ∞

1 3 5 7 9 10 8 6 4 2

The artist used ink line and watercolor on Arches paper
to create the illustrations for this book.

For Alex,
the happy hat man
—E. W.

For Alex, Abby,
Michael, and James
—S. T.

Floppy hats and sloppy hats,
silly hats and frilly hats.

Flowered hats for bees to buzz in,
fussy hats from someone's cousin.

Hats to cover up your toes
(those are socks as everyone knows).

Pinwheel hats and paper hats,

tall black hats to wear with spats.

Hats for queens with diamonds bright,
hats for brides all dressed in white.

Hats for fancy race-car drivers,

hats with air for deep-sea divers.

Big straw hats with ribbons flying,
smashed-on hats for secret spying.

Peek-a-boo hats if baby's crying,

flyaway hats with strings for tying.

Hats with feathers,
hats with ears,

hats to wave when someone cheers.

Hats to save you when you fall,

hats to make you very tall,

big fat hats to shrink you small.

Miners' hats with lamps that light,
hats for guards who work at night.

Hats with flaps, hats with braids,
hats for generals in parades.

Hats to wear across home plate,
hats for hair that sticks up straight.

March right in,

it's HALLOWEEN NIGHT!

Make a circle,
shout your name,
it's time to play
a switching game.

Snatch your hat right off your hair,
throw it high up in the air,
catch some other falling hat,
put this one on instead of that.

Now skip away,
be someone new . . .

. . . let your hat tell you who.